NBA HOT STREAKS

BY EMMA HUDDLESTON

Published by The Child's World®
1980 Lookout Drive • Mankato, MN 56003-1705
800-599-READ • www.childsworld.com

Photographs ©: Jeff Chiu/AP Images, cover, 1;
Tony Dejak/AP Images, 5; AP Images, 6, 9; WGI/
AP Images, 10; Red Line Editorial, 12; Rusty
Kennedy/AP Images, 13; G. Paul Burnett/AP
Images, 14; Focus On Shot/Getty Images Sport/
Getty Images, 16; Al Messerschmidt Archive/
AP Images, 18, 21; John Swart/AP Images, 22;
Charles Bennett/AP Images, 23; Ben Margot/AP
Images, 24; Tyler Kaufman/AP Images, 26; Kamil
Krzaczynski/AP Images, 28

Copyright © 2020 by The Child's World®
All rights reserved. No part of this book may be
reproduced or utilized in any form or by any means
without written permission from the publisher.

ISBN 9781503832275
LCCN 2018963087

Printed in the United States of America
PA02422

ABOUT THE AUTHOR

Emma Huddleston lives in Minnesota with her husband. She enjoys writing children's books, but she likes reading novels even more. When she is not writing or reading, she likes to stay active by running, hiking, or swing dancing.

CONTENTS

FAST FACTS 4

CHAPTER ONE
Chamberlain's 100 Points 7

CHAPTER TWO
Piling Up the Wins 11

CHAPTER THREE
Smith's 17 Blocks 15

CHAPTER FOUR
Jordan in the 1993 NBA Finals 19

CHAPTER FIVE
Three-Point Hot Streaks 25

Think About It 29
Glossary 30
Source Notes 31
To Learn More 32
Index 32

FAST FACTS

Regular Season and Postseason

▶ In the National Basketball Association (NBA) regular season, each team plays 82 games. They play 41 games at home and 41 games away. At the end of the regular season, the top eight teams in each **conference** (Western Conference and Eastern Conference) make the playoffs. The final two teams meet in the NBA Finals.

Game Rules

▶ Each NBA game is 48 minutes long and is broken up into four 12-minute quarters.

▶ Five players from each team are on the court at a time.

▶ The 24-second shot clock was introduced in the 1954–55 season to make the game more fast-paced. If the clock ran out before the team on offense took a shot at the basket, then the ball would be turned over to the other team.

▶ The three-point line was established for the 1979–80 season, and it continued into future seasons.

The Golden State Warriors and the Cleveland Cavaliers ▶ faced off in the 2018 NBA Finals. The Warriors won.

CHAPTER ONE

CHAMBERLAIN'S 100 POINTS

It was halftime, and Wilt Chamberlain had played every minute of the game so far. He was sweating. His Philadelphia Warriors jersey clung to his skin. But Chamberlain didn't care because he was on a hot streak. He had already scored 41 points, and he wanted his team to win this 1962 game against the New York Knicks. But it was a close competition. Before going back out onto the court, Chamberlain got a drink of water in the locker room. He didn't want to lose his momentum in the second half.

Playing defense against Chamberlain was not easy. He was over 7 feet (2 m) tall and weighed more than 250 pounds (113 kg). One Knicks defender tried to stop Chamberlain from dribbling toward the hoop. Chamberlain shot the ball over the defender and into the basket. Chamberlain had scored more than 70 points at that point in the fourth quarter.

◀ **In the 1961-62 season, Wilt Chamberlain scored an average of just over 50 points each game.**

By the third and fourth quarters, Chamberlain was busy at the free-throw line, too. The Knicks were **fouling** him because they were frustrated with how much he was scoring. But instead of getting angry when he was fouled, Chamberlain took a deep breath and stayed calm. He stepped up to the free-throw line and looked at the basket. There was noise all around him, so he had to focus. Each point mattered. Chamberlain made another free throw and grinned. His teammate slapped him on the shoulder. The Warriors were winning, and Chamberlain's streak continued.

Forty-six seconds remained. The crowd was chanting, "Give it to Wilt! Give it to Wilt!"[1] With sweat dripping down his forehead, Chamberlain looked to his teammate for a pass. The ball hit Chamberlain's palms, and then he looked to the basket.

WILT "THE STILT"

Over time, Chamberlain put on muscle, so he weighed more than 300 pounds (136 kg). He jumped higher and used his strength against tough defenses. People also commented on how tall he was. He got the nickname "the Stilt" because of his size.[2] Some people even called him "the Big Dipper" because he had to dip his head under doorways.[3] Chamberlain was able to use his size and strength to score a lot of points.

▲ **Chamberlain (13) scored more than 31,000 points during his basketball career.**

He raised his arms and released the ball. It spun through the air and dropped through the hoop. He did it! Chamberlain scored 100 points, easily setting the NBA record for the most points in a game. In that historic game, the Warriors beat the Knicks 169–147. This hot streak became Chamberlain's legacy, and the NBA record has lasted for more than 50 years.

CHAPTER TWO

PILING UP THE WINS

The Baltimore Bullets and the Los Angeles Lakers faced off on November 5, 1971. At halftime, the Lakers were ahead by two points. The score was 58–56. The players jogged off the court and into the locker rooms. Gail Goodrich was a shooting guard for the Lakers. He grabbed a bottle and squirted cold water into his mouth. Some dripped down to his jersey. He wanted to get back onto the court. The game was close during the second half, but the Lakers won 110–106. This was the first game of their famous 33-game winning streak.

The Lakers worked together as a team to defeat many **opponents**. Goodrich played in every game. He loved walking onto the court and hearing the familiar sounds of a basketball game. There were fans clapping in the background.

◄ **Gail Goodrich was a key player for the Lakers during their hot streak.**

His teammates' shoes squeaked on the hardwood floor, and the game buzzer rang on the court.

The Lakers won 14 games in November and continued with 16 wins in December. Goodrich said, "We were really just having fun. I don't think we really realized what we were doing."[4]

WINNING STREAKS

SEASON	TEAM	STREAK
1971–72	LA Lakers	33 games
2014–15 and 2015–16	Golden State Warriors	28 games
2012–13	Miami Heat	27 games
2007–08	Houston Rockets	22 games
1970–71	Milwaukee Bucks	20 games
1999–2000	LA Lakers	19 games
2008–09	Boston Celtics	19 games
2013–14	San Antonio Spurs	19 games
2014–15	Atlanta Hawks	19 games

▲ **Goodrich tried to stop a play by the Philadelphia 76ers.**

On December 12, they won their 21st **consecutive** game. That broke a record set by the Milwaukee Bucks one year earlier. The Lakers' streak had reached 33 wins by the time they traveled to Milwaukee to play the Bucks on January 9, 1972. At halftime, Milwaukee was winning 51–45. The Lakers felt pressure to keep their winning streak alive. Going into the last quarter, the Lakers were down by seven points, and they needed to fight back. They gave it their best effort, but the Bucks beat the Lakers 120–104 and ended Los Angeles' winning streak at 33 games. Even though the Lakers lost, they were proud to have had the longest winning streak in NBA history. When Goodrich reflected on the Lakers' impressive winning streak, he said, "I've always said records are meant to be broken. This one, I'm not so sure."[5]

CHAPTER THREE

SMITH'S 17 BLOCKS

The crowd was cheering with their hands in the air. Elmore Smith had his hands up, too, but for a different reason. He was preparing to block one of his opponent's shots. Before the ball left his opponent's hands, Smith jumped and reached for it. When the ball slapped his hand, he knew he had done his job. Smith was on defense, and he successfully stopped the other team from scoring. On October 26, 1973, Smith set the NBA record for most blocks in one game, with 14. But that record lasted only two days.

On October 28, 1973, Smith's Lakers played the Portland Trail Blazers. Smith laced up his shoes and put on his Lakers jersey to prepare for the game. He was in the starting lineup, so he walked out onto the court and waited for the whistle to screech. During the first half, Smith blocked several shots.

◄ **The Lakers traded Elmore Smith (left) in 1975. Smith played for the Cleveland Cavaliers from 1977 to 1979.**

▲ **Smith jumps to block a shot against a Bullets player in 1973.**

When he saw a Trail Blazer preparing to shoot, he bent his knees and pushed off the ground into the air. He raised one hand high above his head, and he aimed for the ball. Bam! Each time he made a block, he knew he was playing good defense.

Smith protected the basket by staying close to it and using his size against his opponents. When he was guarding someone, he set his feet wide and leaned into his opponent with his chest.

Once another player picked up the ball, Smith locked his eyes on his opponent. Smith saw his opponent start to shift. His shoulder muscles tensed, and he bent his knees to jump. The ball was released into the air. Smith knew just where to reach his hand. When he felt the ball smack his hand, he knew he had stopped another shot.

Smith later said, "I didn't realize how many I blocked until after the game."[6] He blocked 17 shots that night and broke his own record. At the start of the 2018–19 season, Smith's 1973 defensive streak against the Trail Blazers was still the NBA all-time record for most blocks in one game.

RECORDING BLOCKS

Bill Russell left a defensive legacy in the NBA. He played from 1956 to 1969 and helped the Boston Celtics win 11 championships in 13 seasons. He intimidated players by blocking their shots and **rebounding** when they missed a basket. He was an impressive defensive player and ended his NBA career with 21,620 rebounds. Russell played before blocks were recorded. The first year the NBA officially counted blocks in a player's statistics was 1973. No one knows how many Russell might have had.

CHAPTER FOUR

JORDAN IN THE 1993 NBA FINALS

Michael Jordan seemed to be floating as he hung in the air. He sensed the precise split second when he needed to release the ball. It fell through the net. One of Jordan's teammates slapped him on the back. It was as if he couldn't miss. The Chicago Bulls' star was averaging more than 42 points per game so far in the NBA Finals. It was a record-setting pace. Now, if the Bulls could beat the Phoenix Suns in Game 6, they'd be NBA champions.

One of Jordan's teammates stole the ball from the Suns. He made a quick pass to Jordan. Jordan dribbled the ball down the court, just inside the three-point line. He took two huge steps toward the hoop and flicked his wrist. The ball went in. He was on another scoring streak. A moment later, the Suns scored. It was a close game, and at halftime the Bulls were only up by five points.

◄ **Michael Jordan was drafted by the Chicago Bulls in 1984.**

19

The score was 56–51. Jordan wiped the sweat off his forehead. He knew the whole team had to work together to stay ahead and win the NBA title.

By the fourth quarter, with just two minutes and 20 seconds left, the Suns were winning 98–94. Jordan tried to focus on the game despite the noise of the crowd. With less than one minute on the clock, the Bulls were on defense. Jordan got a rebound and started dribbling. He knew every second counted. When he looked down the court, he saw an open path to the basket. He moved quickly and scored a **layup**. The Bulls were still behind by two points with only 38 seconds left in the game.

A SUPERSTAR

Jordan is called "the greatest basketball player of all time" and an "NBA superstar" by basketball fans and experts.[7] But years earlier, he had been cut from his high school varsity basketball team. However, Jordan did not let that stop him from playing the sport he loved. He continued to practice and made the team as a junior. Then he played basketball at the University of North Carolina. At the end of his career in 2003, Jordan had the NBA all-time record for the highest scoring average. He averaged 30.1 points per game throughout his career.

▲ Jordan won six NBA championships during his basketball career.

▲ **Jordan poses with his 1993 MVP trophy.**

The Bulls got the ball again, and John Paxson made a three-point shot to put the Bulls in the lead with 3.9 seconds left. The final score was 99–98. The Bulls had won the 1993 NBA championship, and Jordan was the Finals MVP. He scored 33 points in the game against the Suns, and he averaged 41 points per game in the NBA Finals series. This gave him the NBA record for the highest points-per-game average in a Finals series.

◀ **Jordan's ability to hang in the air showed during the 1988 Slam Dunk Contest.**

CHAPTER FIVE

THREE-POINT HOT STREAKS

Stephen Curry wiped his hands on his shirt and took another practice shot. He spent many hours working on his **technique**. He played for the Golden State Warriors, and his signature move was making three-point baskets. One day in 2016, Curry spent extra time working on his three-point shot because he hadn't made any during the game the night before. The gymnasium was warm. Curry walked across the hardwood gymnasium floor and sat on the bench with the ball in his lap. He was determined to get back to making three-pointers in the next game.

Two days later, the Golden State Warriors played the New Orleans Pelicans. Five minutes into the game, Curry got open outside the three-point line. His teammate passed him the ball. Curry focused on the hoop and flicked the ball off his fingertips.

◀ **Stephen Curry has been playing basketball since he was five years old.**

▲ Curry joined the Warriors in 2009.

The ball fell through the net, and Curry's shooting touch was back. His hard work in practice had paid off. He said, "I had another level of focus the last two days trying to get my rhythm back and see the ball go in."[8] Curry's shooting technique was perfect, and he began a hot streak.

Curry made another three-point basket, and another. He made five three-pointers and looked at the clock. He knew he could make one more before halftime. He got a pass from his teammate and looked across the court. Two Pelicans defenders were coming toward him. He dribbled between them and launched another three-point shot. The ball went in for the sixth time. After halftime, Curry's hot streak continued. When the ball rolled off his fingers each time, he had his eyes locked on the basket. The ball flew through the air in a smooth arc and went in. Curry made four three-point baskets in the third quarter.

THREE-POINT MASTER

Curry's hot streak extended beyond the game against the Pelicans. During the 2015–16 season, Curry set the NBA all-time record for the most three-pointers in one season. He made 402 three-point baskets throughout the year. That season, the Golden State Warriors won 73 out of 82 games.

▲ **Curry and Thompson celebrate during the October game against the Bulls.**

The Warriors kept passing Curry the ball. He had ten three-pointers so far, as well as points from free throws and other baskets. In less than two minutes, Curry made three quick three-point shots. On his 13th one, Curry pumped his fist in excitement after it went in. He knew he had just set the NBA record for scoring the most three-point baskets in one game. The Warriors won 116–106, and fans chanted at Curry, "M-V-P! M-V-P!"[9]

However, in 2018 Curry's record was beaten by his own teammate, Klay Thompson. The Warriors faced the Chicago Bulls one October night, and Thompson was ready to shine. "I just knew I was due for a big night," he said. "I just knew it."[10] He started racking up three-pointers, and by halftime he had already made 10, tying the NBA record for three-pointers in a half. Later, the crowd jumped to its feet and gave Thompson a loud **ovation** when his 14th three-pointer went through the hoop to beat Curry's record. And Curry was proud of his teammate, saying, "Records are obviously meant to be broken. I'm just happy it's my teammate and nobody else. And I got to witness it in person."[11] The Warriors beat the Bulls 149–124 that night.

THINK ABOUT IT

► Which hot streak do you think is most impressive? Explain your answer.
► How can teams work together to play basketball? Why do you think it's important for teams to work together?
► How is playing basketball different from playing other sports? How are the rules and the season different? How are they similar?

GLOSSARY

conference (KAHN-fur-uhns): A conference is a group of teams. The NBA is divided into the Eastern Conference and Western Conference.

consecutive (kuhn-SEK-yuh-tiv): Consecutive means it happened in a row. The Lakers are famous for winning 33 consecutive games.

fouling (FOWL-ing): Fouling occurs when an opponent makes illegal contact with a player. The Knicks kept fouling Chamberlain.

layup (LAY-uhp): A layup is a shot in basketball made from near the basket. Jordan scored an important layup for the Bulls in the 1993 NBA Finals.

opponents (uh-POH-nuhntz): Opponents are players or teams you are competing against. Basketball teams work together to defeat their opponents.

ovation (oh-VAY-shun): An ovation is a show of excitement from a crowd of people that can involve clapping and cheering. Thompson got a loud ovation.

rebounding (REE-bownd-ing): Rebounding is getting the ball after a missed basket. Smith and Russell were impressive defensive players who were known for rebounding the ball.

technique (tek-NEEK): Technique is a way of doing something with skill. Curry is known for having a great shooting technique.

SOURCE NOTES

1. "Wilt Scores 100!" *NBA*. NBA Media Ventures, n.d. Web. 13 Dec. 2018.

2. "Chamberlain Bio." *NBA*. NBA Media Ventures, n.d. Web. 13 Dec. 2018.

3. Ibid.

4. J. A. Adande. "The Greatest Streak in NBA History." *ESPN*. ESPN Internet Ventures, 28 Mar. 2013. Web. 13 Dec. 2018.

5. Ibid.

6. Jerry Crowe. "There's One Memory of His NBA Career that Elmore Smith Won't Ever Block Out." *Los Angeles Times*. Los Angeles Times, 14 Nov. 2010. Web. 13 Dec. 2018.

7. "Legends Profile: Michael Jordan." *NBA*. NBA Media Ventures, n.d. Web. 13 Dec. 2018.

8. Janie McCauley. "Stephen Curry Hits NBA-Record 13 3-Pointers." *NBA*. NBA Media Ventures, 8 Nov. 2016. Web. 13 Dec. 2018.

9. Ibid.

10. Nick Friedell. "Klay Thompson on Record 14 3s: 'Just Knew I Was Due for a Big Night.'" *ESPN*. ESPN Internet Ventures, 30 Oct. 2018. Web. 13 Dec. 2018.

11. Ibid.

TO LEARN MORE

BOOKS

Aaseng, Nathan. *Michael Jordan: Hall of Fame Basketball Superstar.* Berkeley Heights, NJ: Enslow Publishing, 2014.

Buckley, James, Jr. *Scholastic Year in Sports 2018.* New York, NY: Scholastic, 2017.

Zuckerman, Gregory. *Rising Above: How 11 Athletes Overcame Challenges in Their Youth to Become Stars.* New York, NY: Philomel Books, 2016.

WEBSITES

Visit our website for links about the NBA: **childsworld.com/links**

Note to Parents, Teachers, and Librarians: We routinely verify our Web links to make sure they are safe and active sites. So encourage your readers to check them out!

INDEX

Chamberlain, Wilt, 7–9
Chicago Bulls, 19–20, 23, 29
Curry, Stephen, 25, 27–29

Golden State Warriors, 25, 27–29
Goodrich, Gail, 11–13

Jordan, Michael, 19–20, 23

layup, 20
Los Angeles Lakers, 11–13, 15

Philadelphia Warriors, 7–9

rebound, 17, 20
Russell, Bill, 17

Smith, Elmore, 15–17

Thompson, Klay, 29